Everything YOU

Elizabeth McPike

PICTURES BY Jay Fleck

FARRAR STRAUS GIROUX
NEW YORK

For Alina Gabriela,
blessed, loved, always —E.M.

To Audrey and Owen,
who are everything to me —J.F.

Farrar Straus Giroux Books for Young Readers
An imprint of Macmillan Publishing Group, LLC
175 Fifth Avenue, New York 10010

Printed in China by RR Donnelley Asia Printing Solutions Ltd.,
Dongguan City, Guangdong Province
Designed by Kristie Radwilowicz
First edition, 2017
10 9 8 7 6 5 4 3 2 1

mackids.com

Library of Congress Cataloging-in-Publication Data

Names: McPike, Elizabeth, author. | Fleck, Jay, illustrator.
Title: Everything you / Elizabeth McPike ; pictures by Jay Fleck.
Description: First edition. | New York : Farrar Straus Giroux, 2017. |
    Summary: "A mother and father welcome a new baby into their lives"—
    Provided by publisher.
Identifiers: LCCN 2016058776 | ISBN 9780374301415 (hardcover)
Subjects: | CYAC: Stories in rhyme. | Babies—Fiction. | Parent and
    child—Fiction.
Classification: LCC PZ8.3.M46175 Eve 2017 | DDC [E]—dc23
LC record available at https://lccn.loc.gov/2016058776

Our books may be purchased in bulk for promotional, educational,
or business use. Please contact your local bookseller or the
Macmillan Corporate and Premium Sales Department
at (800) 221-7945 ext. 5442 or by e-mail at
MacmillanSpecialMarkets@macmillan.com.

We wait and we wait,
we watch all day through,
and our dreams while we wait
are of **EVERYTHING YOU**.

You're everything HOPEFUL,
the world starts anew,

You're everything **CUDDLY**,
our hush-a-bye you.

You're everything FRESH,
the morning's first dew,

You're everything **GROWING**,
our summertime you.

You're everything **DADDY**,
 your fur the same hue,

You're everything **MOMMY**,
   our Valentine you.

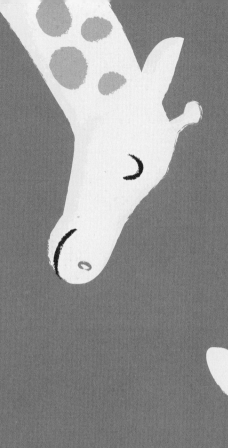

You're everything LiTTLE,
wee sock and wee shoe,

You're everything **PLAYFUL**,
our peek-a-boo you.

You're everything **KISSES**,
two hundred you blew,

You're everything **GENTLE**,
our cottontail you.

You're everything **MUSIC,**

skip, skip to my Lou,

You're every **HAPPY ENDING**,
our fairy-tale you.

You're everything WONDROUS,
the stars and moon knew,

You're everything POSSIBLE,
our miracle you.

You're every wish answered,
our hearts, how they grew . . .
every day countless,
EVERYTHING YOU.